Sofia the First

Sofia's Royal World

By Andrea Posner-Sanchez

Illustrated by Grace Lee and the Disney Storybook Art Team

 A GOLDEN BOOK • NEW YORK

Copyright © 2014 Disney Enterprises, Inc. *The Perfect Tea Party* copyright © 2013 Disney Enterprises, Inc.
Bunny Magic © 2014 Disney Enterprises, Inc. All rights reserved. Published in the United States by Golden Books,
an imprint of Random House Children's Books, a division of Random House LLC, 1745 Broadway, New York, NY
10019, and in Canada by Random House of Canada Limited, Toronto, Penguin Random House Companies,
in conjunction with Disney Enterprises, Inc. Golden Books, A Golden Book, A Big Golden Book, the G colophon,
and the distinctive gold spine are registered trademarks of Random House LLC.
randomhouse.com/kids
ISBN 978-0-7364-3262-7
Printed in the United States of America
10 9 8 7 6 5 4 3 2 1

A ROYAL MEETING

Introducing Sofia and her friends and family from Enchancia!

Princess Sofia

Sofia wasn't born a princess. This kind and clever eight-year-old recently became royalty when her mother married King Roland II. Sofia loves exploring the kingdom and staying in touch with her friends from the village.

Sofia's stepsister, Amber, is the daughter of the king, so she is used to living in a castle and being a princess. Amber gets along fine with Sofia—but she sometimes wishes she were still the only princess of Enchancia.

Princess Amber

Prince James

James is Amber's twin brother and Sofia's stepbrother. He loves to play pranks and have fun. His sisters have a hard time believing that one day James will be crowned king of Enchancia!

Baileywick is the Castle Steward. He has worked in the castle ever since King Roland II was a little boy. If any of the royals needs something taken care of, Baileywick will get it done!

Sofia's mother, Miranda, owned a shoe store in the village before she married the king. She is a very caring queen who looks out for the castle's servants and loves her new stepchildren, Amber and James.

Clover is Sofia's best friend in the castle. This bunny loves spending time with the princess—especially if there's food involved! Sofia is able to talk to Clover, and all other animals in the kingdom, thanks to a magical amulet given to her by the king.

Cedric is the Royal Sorcerer. He lives and works in the castle tower with his pet raven, Wormwood. Cedric isn't a very skilled sorcerer—his magic spells don't always work. That's a good thing, because Cedric's dream is to swipe Sofia's amulet and use its power to take over the kingdom!

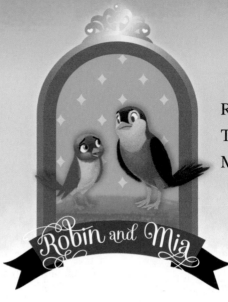

Robin and Mia are two songbirds who live in the woodlands. They're often found spending time with Clover the rabbit. Mia is a bluebird and Robin is a robin.

Minimus is a purple flying pony. He is Sofia's partner on her school's Flying Derby team and is always available when the princess needs to fly somewhere in a hurry.

Crackle is a cute little dragon who has a big crush on Clover. The bunny needs to be careful—Crackle tends to breathe fire when she gets excited!

Jade and Ruby are Sofia's best friends from the village. Even though Sofia lives in the castle now, she always makes time for her old friends.

The Perfect Tea Party

Based on the script "Tea for Too Many"
by Doug Cooney

Illustrated by Grace Lee

It's an exciting day at Royal Prep—the fairies are choosing which student will host the annual school tea party.

Sofia's new stepsister, Amber, explains that Royal Prep tea parties are really big events. "They have merry-go-rounds, ponies, and even hot-air balloons!"

Sofia has never been to a royal tea party. She just recently became a princess when her mother married King Roland.

In class, Sofia's teacher, Flora, holds out a teapot.
"Only students who haven't had a chance to host a party
should submit their names," says the fairy.
Sofia excitedly drops a slip of paper
with her name on it into the teapot.

Flora uses her wand to stir the pot. Soon one paper magically floats out.

"The host of the next Royal Prep tea party will be . . . Princess Sofia!" she announces.

Sofia is thrilled.

"You can throw any kind of party you like," Flora tells her. "This is your chance to show us who you are."

On the ride home from school, Sofia talks about the tea party with Amber and her stepbrother, James. "There have already been so many big, fancy tea parties," she says. "I'd like to throw a simple tea party like I used to in the village. My friends and I would spread blankets on the ground and borrow teacups from our mothers."

James thinks that sounds cool. Amber doesn't. "No one wants to use borrowed teacups!" she exclaims. "When it comes to royal parties, the bigger the better!"

Sofia starts to think that maybe Amber is right. She spots the swan fountain and tells Baileywick, the castle caretaker, that she would like to have a swan-themed tea party. "We'll have swan-shaped cookies and cakes."

"That sounds lovely," says Baileywick. Amber likes the swan theme but encourages Sofia to think even bigger.

"Hmm. Maybe Cedric, the Royal Sorcerer, can make the tables and chairs float in the air like swans float on water," suggests Sofia. "And the swans can put on a show."

"That's more like it!" says Amber.

Later that day, Sofia is visited by her friends from the village, Jade and Ruby. Even though Sofia is busy planning the Royal Prep tea party, she is happy to take a break to spend time with them.

"Let's have a little snack," Sofia suggests. "I know the perfect spot."

Sofia leads Jade and Ruby along a row of hedges. Then she pushes aside some ivy, uncovering a wooden door. The door opens and the girls step into Sofia's secret garden.

"It's beautiful!" says Ruby.

"Look at all the butterflies!" cries Jade.

The girls spread out a blanket and share a plate of cookies. "This reminds me of the tea parties we had in the village," Ruby says. "Are you throwing a party like this for your princess friends?"

Sofia sighs. "I want to, but they expect a big, fancy tea party."

"That's too bad, because I'm having a great time just doing this," says Ruby.

"Me too," agrees Sofia.

After a few more cookies, Sofia sadly says good-bye and gets back to her party planning.

"Ah, Princess Sofia, you're just in time to choose the plates for your party," Baileywick says as Sofia enters the dining room.

Sofia looks at all the choices. She likes the simple white ones.

Amber shakes her head and holds up a large, shiny golden plate. "You need something like this," she declares. "Remember, bigger is better."

Sofia gives in and agrees to use the large golden plates.

At another table, James is happily munching on a swan-shaped cookie. "These are great!" he declares as crumbs fall from his mouth.

"You should order two hundred of these cookies for the tea party, and make them as big as possible," Amber tells Sofia. "You'll need a huge swan cake, too!"

Sofia thinks it's too much, but she listens to Amber anyway.

Next, Sofia heads to Cedric's workshop.

"I'm hosting a tea party tomorrow, and it would be great if you could make all the tables and chairs rise just a little bit off the ground," Sofia explains to the Royal Sorcerer. "Do you have a spell that can do that?"

Floaticus - hover - a - boo !

Cedric points his wand at a beaker on his worktable. "Floaticus-hover-a-boo!" The beaker twinkles magically and rises into the air.

"That's terrific!" cries Sofia. "See you at the party tomorrow."

Sofia goes to the swan fountain. Luckily, the magical amulet King Roland gave her, the Amulet of Avalar, gives her the power to talk to animals!

"I'm hosting a tea party, and I was hoping you could perform a water ballet," she tells the swans.

"It would be our pleasure," replies Portia.

"Great! See you tomorrow!" says Sofia, and rushes off to find the perfect tea party dress.

As the royal dressmaker hems her gown, Sofia tells her
mother about the tea party. "It is going to be so big and fancy.
Amber says everyone is going to love it." She sighs. "But part of
me wishes I could just have a sweet tea party like the ones I used
to have with Ruby and Jade."

"I'm sure everyone will be pleased no matter what kind of
party you throw," says Queen Miranda.

The day of Sofia's royal tea party has arrived! As the servants rush about, everything goes wrong. The swan-shaped ice sculpture falls off its cart and slides into the baker, who drops his tray of swan cookies. Then the ice slides into the fountain, scaring the swans.

The swans fly into Cedric just as he is casting his floating spell! The tables and chairs rise off the ground—and float away! Sofia can't believe her eyes!

The princess regrets listening to Amber. Her party is ruined, and the guests are on their way. Sofia starts to cry. Then she spots a butterfly and knows exactly what to do.

When the students and fairies arrive, Baileywick moves aside some ivy, pushes open the wooden door, and welcomes them into Sofia's secret garden. Blankets on the grass have been set with teapots and cups. Butterflies flutter over the flowers. And all the princesses love it—including Amber!

"Nice job, Sofia! I guess bigger isn't always better," Amber admits.

"Princess Sofia, what a charming party!" Flora tells the hostess. "Some peppermint tea, a pretty garden, and a beautiful view. Who could ask for more?"

All the guests raise their teacups and cheer, "To Princess Sofia!"

Sofia is pleased to learn that even princesses can enjoy simple things. She giggles and raises her own teacup. "Hooray for me!"

TEA FOR YOU!

You can throw a tea party just like Sofia did. Place a tablecloth or a blanket on the floor and invite friends, relatives, or even your favorite stuffed animals over for a tea-rific time.

Special Sips

Just because it's called a tea party, don't think you have to serve tea! You can have lemonade, milk, or a special royal fruit punch instead. To make the punch, ask an adult to help you mix equal parts orange juice and pineapple juice with a little bit of grenadine or pomegranate juice. It tastes—and looks—great!

Princess Nibbles

Need a royal snack to go with your royal tea? Mini sandwiches are fun to eat and fun to make—just ask an adult for help, and follow these simple steps:

1. Remove the crust from your favorite kind of bread.
2. Spread on jam, cream cheese, peanut butter, or any other filling you like.
3. Top with another slice of bread.
4. Use cookie cutters to make the sandwiches into shapes. You can even make swan-shaped sandwiches to match Sofia's party theme!

Sweet Endings

Instead of serving cookies and cupcakes, try fruit salad in an ice cream cone! Simply fill a flat-bottomed cone with cut-up pieces of your favorite fruit, and you have a special treat that's also good for you!

Royal Fun

Invite your guests to make their own one-of-a-kind jewelry. String pieces of O-shaped cereal onto ribbon to make bracelets and necklaces. After a tea-party fashion show, everyone can eat their edible "jewels"!

BUNNY MAGIC!

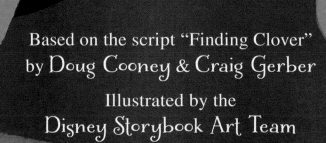

Based on the script "Finding Clover"
by Doug Cooney & Craig Gerber

Illustrated by the
Disney Storybook Art Team

It's a lovely day in Enchancia. Princess Sofia and her pet bunny, Clover, are playing hide-and-seek in the royal vegetable garden. Suddenly, Sofia notices a pile of radishes that seems to be moving. "Found you!" Sofia cries. "That was good—until you started to eat your hiding place," she adds with a giggle.

"Okay, Princess," says Clover. "Now it's your turn to hide."

"I wish I could, but I don't have time," Sofia replies as she heads off to archery class.

The next day, Clover and Sofia watch a magic show together. Clover's favorite part is when a rabbit named Mr. Cuddles magically appears.

After the show, Clover hops in front of the princess and announces, "Now I, the Amazing Clover, am about to take you on an afternoon of adventure!"

Just then, Minimus the flying pony arrives to take Sofia to Flying Derby practice.

"Sorry, Clover," says the princess as she puts on her riding outfit. "We'll do something later, okay?"

Robin and Mia swoop down to cheer Clover up as he sadly watches Sofia and Minimus fly away.

Clover perks up a bit when he notices Mr. Cuddles hop by. "Hey, great show!" he calls to the magician's rabbit.

"Thanks, but I'm quitting," replies Mr. Cuddles. "I want to be a serious actor, not a magician's prop. You want the job? It's yours."

Clover thinks being a magic rabbit sounds like fun. "And anyway, Sofia will be too busy to even notice I'm gone," he tells Robin and Mia. The little birds try to convince Clover to stay, but his mind is made up. He jumps on the magician's wagon. "Farewell!" he says as it rolls out the kingdom gates.

The next morning, Sofia is surprised to find Clover's bed empty.

"He joined the magic show," Robin tells the princess. "He said you didn't need him around anymore."

Sofia is stunned. "That's not true!" she exclaims. "I've got to find Clover and ask him to come home!" She puts on her riding clothes and rushes to the stable.

Sofia asks Minimus to help her find Clover. Crackle wants to go, too. "You never know when a dragon will come in handy!" Crackle says.

The friends zoom through the sky, searching the roads for a red covered wagon.

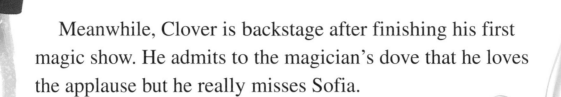

Meanwhile, Clover is backstage after finishing his first magic show. He admits to the magician's dove that he loves the applause but he really misses Sofia.

"Hey, I left some friends behind, too," the dove tells Clover. "But this is better. We're big stars now!"

Clover isn't sure he agrees.

A little later, Sophia, Minimus, and Crackle land near a red covered wagon. "Oh, it's not the magician," Sofia says sadly when she spots a woman with a crystal ball.

"I am better than a magician!" announces the woman. "I am Madame Ubetcha, the greatest fortune-teller!"

Sofia tells Madame Ubetcha that they are looking for her pet rabbit. The fortune-teller peers into her crystal ball and says, "Crystal ball, don't be funny. Help me find this girl's bunny!" Suddenly, an image of Clover appears inside the glowing ball. Next to him is a fancy tower.

"I've seen that tower before!" declares Sofia. "It's in Somerset Village."

"Let's go! Let's go!" cries Crackle.

After thanking the fortune-teller, the friends race off.

Meanwhile, Clover has been telling the dove story after story about his friend Sofia.

"Hey, kid," the dove interrupts, "if you two had so much fun together, why did you leave?"

"She got busy and didn't have time for me," Clover admits.

"Most people get busy," replies the dove. "That doesn't mean they love you any less."

"I'm going home," Clover says, and he hops toward the exit door.

But the magician stops him. "I'm not about to have another bunny run out on me," he says, stuffing Clover into his hat. "Five minutes till showtime!"

"Clover!"

After the magician goes onstage, Clover hears a friendly voice call his name.

"I've been looking for you everywhere!" exclaims Sofia. "I'm sorry I wasn't spending enough time with you. If you come back, I'll make it up to you."

Clover leaps into Sofia's arms for a hug.

Then the magician returns. "What are you doing with my magic bunny?" he demands, snatching Clover from Sofia. "If you want to see him, feel free to buy a ticket to the show."

Clover's eyes fill with tears as he is put back into the hat and carried onstage.

Luckily, Sofia has seen this magic act before—and she comes up with a plan. "All I need to do is volunteer for the last trick and Clover will appear right in my arms!" she tells her friends. "But I need a disguise."

Madame Ubetcha suddenly appears, holding out a yellow cloak. "I *knew* you would need this," the fortune-teller says.

Sofia pulls the hood of the cloak over her head. She finds a seat in the audience just as the magician asks for a volunteer for his grand finale.

The princess raises her hand and calls out, "Me! Me!" in a deep voice. The magician calls her to the stage. Even Clover doesn't recognize her.

"Let the amazement begin!" shouts the magician. He puts Clover in a box and closes the curtain. When the curtain is opened again, Clover is gone!

"Now, young lady," the magician says to Sofia, "it is your turn to step inside."

Sofia steps in. After the curtain is closed, a hidden panel in the box rotates, and Sofia and Clover are together! She takes off her hood and whispers, "I'm here to rescue you!"

The magician pulls back the curtain. He peeks through the back of the box and sees Sofia and Clover running away. "Come back with my magic bunny!" he yells.

Sofia and Clover jump on Minimus's back. But the magician grabs hold of Clover before the pony can take off. Robin and Mia block his path. As the magician turns, Crackle swoops down and lets out a burst of flames. The magician yelps and drops Clover.

Crackle catches the bunny, and his friends cheer. "I told you it would be handy to have a dragon around," Crackle says proudly.

Clover thanks everyone for saving him.

"Next time you have a problem, promise you'll come talk to me before you go off and join a magic show," Sofia tells her furry friend.

"You got it!" replies Clover. Then he cuddles up to Sofia as Minimus flies them back home.

Put on your magic hat and get ready to amaze your family and friends with these simple tricks. Just don't forget to say "Abracadabra!"

The Rubber Pencil

What you need: a pencil

What to do:

1. Pick up the pencil and show it to your audience. Tell them you are going to magically change it into a rubber pencil!
2. Hold the pencil loosely at one end between your thumb and pointer.
3. Shake your fingers and wave the pencil up and down at the same time. The pencil will wobble, making it look as if it is made of rubber!

Instant Ice

What you need: a mug, a sponge, an ice cube, a cup with a little water, a plastic bowl

What to do:

1. Before you gather your audience, put a sponge in the bottom of a mug. Make sure it is wedged in tight and will not fall out if you turn the mug over.
2. Place an ice cube on top of the sponge.
3. Have your audience come in, and tell them that you are going to change water into ice right before their eyes.
4. Carefully pour a little bit of water from the cup into the mug. Then wait for the sponge to soak up the water as you say some magic words.
5. Hold the mug over the bowl and turn it upside down—the ice cube will fall out of the mug. Amazing!

ROYAL HIDE-AND-SEEK

Clover loves playing hide-and-seek with Sofia.
Now you can, too! Here's a fun royal version of the game that
you can play at home. All you need are paper, crayons, and at least
two people.

1. Draw a picture of Princess Sofia on a piece of paper.
2. Choose who will hide and who will seek. There can be more than one seeker at a time, with all the seekers working together.
3. While the seekers close their eyes and count to twenty, the hider hides the picture of Sofia somewhere in the house.
4. When a seeker finds the picture, she becomes the hider and hides Sofia for the next round.

Game Tips

• Agree on which areas are off-limits. For example, no one should hide anything in the oven or near your mom's collection of delicate perfume bottles!
• You can give hints to the seekers by telling them if they are hot or cold. As they get closer to the hiding spot, tell them they are getting warm. When they are right next to the spot, tell them they are hot! If they move away from the new hiding spot, tell them they're getting colder.

Have a royally fun time!